Shall: ghazals

DATE DUE

Shall: ghazals

Catherine Owen

Wolsak and Wynn • Toronto

Cover image: Joe Rosenblatt
Author's photograph: Gary Desjardins
Book design: Julie McNeill/McNeill Design Arts
Typeset in Sabon

Some of these poems have appeared in *Pottersfield Portfolio* and in
Poetry and Spiritual Practice (St Thomas Poetry Series, 02).

The publishers gratefully acknowledge
the support of the Canada Council for
the Arts, the Ontario Arts Council, and
the Book Publishing Industry Development
Program (BPIDP) for their financial
assistance.

The Canada Council | Le Conseil des Arts
for the Arts | du Canada

ONTARIO ARTS COUNCIL
CONSEIL DES ARTS DE L'ONTARIO

Wolsak and Wynn Publishers Ltd
194 Spadina Avenue, Suite 303
Toronto, ON, Canada M5T 2C2
www.wolsakandwynn.ca

Canadian   Patrimoine
Heritage   canadien

Library and Archives Canada Cataloguing in Publication

Owen, Catherine, 1971-
        Shall : Ghazals / Catherine Owen.

Poems.
ISBN 1-894987-08-X

Title.

PS8579.W43S52 2006   C811'.54   C2006-900661.X
Printed in Canada

For Chad Norman, then,
and Frank Bonneville (1974-2003), always

Contents

12
the drive

13
for a marriage

14

15
for Gerald

16
3/4 length

17
son

18
daughter

19
afraid of growing up

20

21
travelling #1

22
travelling #2

23
travelling #3

24

25
from 2000 ft. up

26
on a cricket's thighbone

27
on silence

28
on absence

29

30

31
for John Thompson (1938 – 1976)

32
for my all-too-gullible heart

33
after a panic attack

34
 on catching a glimpse

35
anniversary

portal

Lying in bed. July, 2000. My muscles, sinews, mind, moribund. One minute I had been breakfasting at a Commercial Drive diner, the next I was being dragged to an emergency ward, rolled through CAT scans and released – a conundrum to the medical profession. Something in me had broken. A year of working on my Masters degree, teaching, writing, parenting, helping to run an after-hours club, recuperating from nights wild with thesis or music. Now I could do nothing. Even staring at the ceiling was too much stimulation. The room gathered its unreadable books, its impossible projects around me. Language, for the first time, painful, impenetrable.

*

After two weeks of life syringed from me by
this unexplainable anchoring of limbs, a
flicker. John Thompson's ghazals ghosted
out, assumed shapes of him crumpled at the
cluttered kitchen table in Jolicoeur, staring
down his grief's ready gun barrel. My body,
all at once, sensed this rhythm, had been
reading Stilt Jack for years, but solely with
the mind, the ear. Now, like blood, his
marshy, Meredith and whisky-haunted
ghazals flooded me.

*

Knew of Hafiz. Knew of Ghalib. But their traditional ghazals with their contained couplets, mantras and rhyme schemes, with the oral force of a community behind their chanted refrains and their surety in the eternal, spiritual nature of love were not mine. Thompson, Rich, Webb and others had, respectfully, reclaimed the form's unique ability to weave a mysterious coherence with the threads of disparate images, translating our North American terrain and perspectives through its generously encompassing lens. Lover's exchanges they remain, regardless.

*

Ghazal wants loss. Ghazal loves a wasteland
where the sun has, not quite, set. Ghazal
resists adjectives, similes. Ghazal is this is
that. Ghazal demands allusions because
ghazal is history, lineage, the remembered
face. Ghazal craves the Anglo-Saxon. Ghazal
says – repeat after me: love, dark, light,
shadows, hands, mouth, lips, seed, tears,
scars, flower, seasons, words. Ghazal
withholds. Ghazal, a – rebel, an iconoclast,
clings with all its might to the Newtonian
universe. Ghazal talks to itself. Ghazal has
faith in the simple. Ghazal speaks or doesn't.
Ghazal adores a trinity. Ghazal is obsessive.
Ghazal is obsessive (did I say that yet?).
Ghazal is obsessive.

*

Once I could hold a pen again, I composed
ghazals the entire summer and into Fall.
There were strange, even paradoxical, rules
governing what I was enabled and forbidden
to write within this tender yet fierce form.
Many of the dictums were irrational, quirky,
but real nonetheless. My life was drawn into
them and whittled down, pared away to a
relentless language. A marriage's erosion
traced in ever fainter gestures. Frank
entering, the Muse of many future projects,
his dark eyes slamming. Children grew a bit,
nostalgia too. Parents aged a little. O, and
Jeffers returned – he never entirely leaves –
nor the earth's imperiled reefs and lilies, their
blooming bowed under asphalt, blindness.
Everything in a ghazal and how small it is –
our human preoccupations merely an
iteration of the same sad and ecstatic themes.
A beauty in this. Though, still.

*

May, 2005. At the Kent's house in Cabbagetown. A Persian poet, a man in a perfectly white shirt with shiny jowls, recites me one of his ghazals, lilted, gleaming. Asks me to return the favour. I cannot. Is it because mine do not rhyme, have not clung tightly to the memory? Claim I have had too much to drink, ashamed. Would Thompson have let a slurred tongue prevent him from singing?

*

Joe Rosenblatt only composes sonnets. A Canadian poet writing ghazals? "Nonsense," he booms, "unethical, even sacrilegious."

*

Microsoft Word doesn't recognize the term, ghazal. It offers me polite, befuddled options instead. Was it "hazels" I wanted? "Gazes," perhaps?

*

Kate Braid wants me to pronounce ghazal in the right way, with a "ha" at the start, the "h" slightly curdled beneath the tongue, a vibration deep as the throat's holy cavern. But I have not yet learned that kind of laughter.

Richmond, BC
October/2005

ghazals

1

At a distance, your laughter
reserves its echo in me.

The hummingbird's beak points
faintly to the stars.

Wind blowing too strongly
to say anything about love.

No traffic with the usual gods
: an androgynous kind of promise.

I would tremble forever if, but once,
I held you naked.

2

after an absence from the world

The cat curves beneath
my breast: long illness.

In back alleys, neighbours
abandon their birdcages.

What – only one bloom
on the rose bush!

Merwin's silences lure me to dream
in a full spectrum of white.

Yet again the moth circles, sears
an instant against the light bulb.

Love is not annulled though some
refuse its syllables.

When I call you this time
look to the moon for a mouth.

3

leaving Qualicum Beach
for Joe Rosenblatt

On the fence, a moth and a snail
talk about holes.

Why can't I commit myself
to your hands?

Crushed oyster shells by the grey-shingled shack.
One heron. Always only one.

Yet then again the ocean.
I stop questioning for a moment.

Four boats in the cove.
Three strawberries huddle

in the glass candle holder.
Raw light.

Why, if the only path is evident,
do I hesitate? The deer on the lip

of the golf course turns her eyes towards us.
Now softly. Now with fear.

4

Two crows on a globe of light
If I could dip my pen in their wings.

Cat flattens out the sun
I look again: shadows.

So this is what you mean by absence?
Memory's doorstep melting. A trumpet

from a high windowsill teetering
on the verge of music.

Odin. Freya. Loki.
Those cold obsessions of childhood.

Did you hear that stumbling. Listen.
I have no brief name for my thirst.

alleyway, 8 a.m.
for Goh Poh Seng

The last rooster on Victoria Drive
crows from a dark shed.

In the wake of the garbage truck, rats
and starlings survive. This then,

is what you've always called freedom.
A man, sipping coffee in a stark garden, shouts

at me – *What address are you wanting?*
Asphalt opens its mouth to utter.

Fennel. Bindweed. Forget-me-nots.
The skyline's wounding sharpens.

Raspberries ripen outside fences.
Their wilderness and my tongue.

Engulfed is not a word
we save for love.

8

A bird's shadow drops from the roof
– I am struck by darkness.

Half in love with easeful death
leaves half

to think otherwise. Sun unstinting
on the clover; a man on a park bench

fits a schedule of simply being.
You have misunderstood me; my lips

are not seeds that random. How
can I give you my absence?

The certain transience of a cloud
: I break & break into again.

9

Rare – the sun this bright, less
my dark thoughts.

As a child, a child
tore a dragonfly

from my wonder.
Brave new world – bocce balls

on the lawn, fruit loops on the tongue,
soma on every screen.

A man and his son crawl
downhill together.

You can't stop stroking
a stranger's arm.

Why enumerate my nightmares?
: the slow orbs of daisies;

my mind tearing sightless
through a garden.

10

from an urban sadness

Irretrievable, the poisoning.
This year's tiny harvest.

I bring my hands up to your lips
in silence. Suggest outings for danger,

suggest anything!
I cannot find a season to settle in

where red no longer smells like green.
If your skin is a seed, who is growing it?

Solace in the asphalt's flat line. Solace
in the wires & scars.

What does not rise anymore without grieving.
What does not require memorial.

11

little sleep

Rain to break July
Your face a palimpsest in mine.

A sac of spider's eggs
– the dark still trailing through.

Deceived you? Tell me how.
I have no hands to age in.

Black figs on the paving stones,
a thistle in my mouth.

Some poems are like morning
– their light berates my seeing.

And I cannot find a castle
: this thin suicide of words.

12

the drive
> *For painter Vladimir Mejer (d. July 12/00).*

Where a man becomes a leaf upon the earth,
a parade passes. Undreamed of elsewhere,

this body language! A black child licking cinnamon.
An aged goddess braying Elvis. Your uncle jiving

to Brazilian samba on the coldest night
in July. What home have you bequeathed us?

Dark lilies in cement.
An eye's long division outside pool halls.

This sweet madness shredding through holes until my hands,
my hands, my

hands. Who saw the painter leave?
He folded up his towns.

The sky cannot add the white now
to his gaze.

13

for a marriage
        for C.N.

I speak to myself in the mirror.
Whose strange dark eyes are these?

Cars – their metal tide. Day & night,
sirens. Innocent – gases

twisting in the ether. How
you cannot pass a flower

without stopping
fills me with your scent.

Knotholes in the desk you nailed. Shelley's
beautiful theories. My shadow was not cut

with my hair. Why is your shadow still
so long, you said.

14

The world blurs beyond our bed
: I climb out of myself in the dusk.

A deer's pelvis on the windowsill,
Jack Daniels' and Canadian flags.

There is a strangeness
we never assuage:

your palm in the curve of my flesh.
Are others in my mind's soft lids?

The licking of a wick in the light.
Slip gently between my scars;

I have written deeper stories than these.
Tell me with your breath you're finding me

in this brief, lush place
beyond keeping.

15

for Gerald

The empty, bodiless grains.
In my mind, Mahapatra trembles.

There is only so much a poem can save.
Is there anything saved by a poem?

You come home from work again
tired, your flesh and the endless road welded.

Glass maps sink into the soil. Tin and old paper
your intimates.

There is no other daughter than time,
the tight ache of metal ripening.

Let me burn into your verses
where the godhead is broken by violence.

You have often named me your mirror
– I pray and I pray for rain.

16

(3/4 length)
for Madeleine

Stones of light cast on the carpet.
Words, their terrible sufficiency.

In the convent, all mirrors were sheeted
I cannot remember to weed.

Have you learned how to answer
my violence? In the drizzle, a hummingbird

darkens. My poems refuse your kindness.
You are younger than my very first fear.

17

son
  for Damian

I bore a world when I bore you
They told me – ten fingers & toes!

There are flowers that thrive best in salt
Your quick, insurmountable tears.

Einstein & Hawking your heroes
and many unreachable planets. Laughing,

you plunge into blindness
Yet who would be willing to save you?

The first hair starts piercing your softness.
I hear only your voice in the choir

daughter
for Rachael

How does the body withstand?
Knowledge of an entrance and dwelling.

Your eyes are engaged with the ocean
your hands with the passage of ants.

Until I first held you I feared
there was no tiny mothering left.

Your gods take animated steps
across an earth struck tyrant with screens.

I'm watching you paint your flesh,
wishing for time's sweet lengthening.

How does the body withstand?
As though nothing and everything were words.

afraid of growing up

Again, the seasons collide.
Where is there place for a word?

A snail pulses low in the seed-bed.
I was ancient before I was born.

A city must cease its klaxon
for a worm to arc into the earth.

You make me a disbeliever. You
find me unlike myself. You tell

me I must shed darkness. You wait
while I suture my caul. Trying

to flame amid blossoms
– a child crouches bright in my gut.

Rain interchanges with rain.
Wanting watching & little of world.

20

Smooth, the world's round shoulders
– I drop my lips like knees.

Always meant to give you this silence.
Dancing, ants swarm in patterns until

their wings fall – without suffering.
As a child, I chose lists, talismans. Now

flesh grows too written on
– incantations fail. Touch

the doorknob! The bell, touch
the glass, avoid the wall.

Tomorrow you will not feel their gaze.
Something locked in thin spaces.

Where are those lips alighting?
I still gather your names on a thread.

21

travelling #1
    Hope, BC

Ghost trees inherit the gullies.
The sand of lost snows.

I gnaw over a nightmare from childhood.
Who is left to remember the earth?

Miles upon miles of fences
Wild flowers weighed & graded.

The eagles have left for the cities.
New clouds scratch over the sun.

Thoreau's wilderness grows hungry
– even then, a train whistle severed.

I am sunk in a love made impossible
Brute absence past scraping on flesh.

22

travelling #2

On stumps, silver numbers
– navels of absent need.

A cross among the tumble weed.
One name in all the silence.

A mall's repetition of wares
What you show me I have felled.

Machinery sprouts in a field
A For Sale sign glows.

Will you ask me again about leaving?
Pale arms of water rise.

The death that has already happened
Writing a poem & traveling:

Two ways
of withdrawing time.

23

travelling #3

Such a shock to find
– initials on the underside of a mushroom.

Corrals enclose the land
Clare laments a severed freedom. Amid

Keep Out signs, we turn inward.
From Jeffers' indifferent cliffs,

a transient bloom sputters.
Hard to love anything untouched.

Hard to see Earth for the imprints.
A heron erupts from the reeds,

language blinks in the bones of fish.
I am flesh

more & more often,
a thief less.

24

Tappen, BC

Sour ferment of sawdust.
Crickets ticking in the sun.

Who is it that follows?
Hieroglyphs of grass on your palm,

a spider on the tip of a thistle.
Country/City,   desire

strings me hard between you
– where Virgil & Hesiod differ.

Drops of water engage the road, clouds
shadow scars on the mountain.

Who can deceive me this time?
Such a sound of unnameable birds.

25

from 2000 ft. up
   Salmon Arm, BC

Something splitting at the seams
– the thin, spaced threads of tree farms.

From this height, the earth lists motionless,
the city, tiny ruins.

So many initials on metal! And
a rare, anonymous butterfly.

Do we know of such edges as these?
You have helped me fall from a pebble.

Purple loosestrife & wires.
A tire track sprouts salal.

Far off, a human motor
– the water scars open & close.

26

on a cricket's thighbone
Lumsden, SK

Sage graduates the hills, wind-
burred wheat, does the world

need another prairie poem?
The last kid in the class to pronounce

ocean, the sound that turns away from you.
Yeats & Pound; Yeats & Pound; Yeats & Pound

– an intermarriage whoring the iambic.
Counting landscapes on my fingers,

I find us, terra plenitum,
sleek's topography. Yet

to scan your own life lacks scansion
libido; farrago; the hunt.

A white bull sidles the valley
Sun un-spells reams of loneliness.

27

on silence

In all the world of sirens,
a man with a kite.

Birds tiny as blood
– the cherry tree scarcely quivers.

You keep asking for my name
The syllables too strange

an answer. Even here.
Even on the mountain. Who

can let absence flesh around them
for an instant? Since Darwin,

slow, unaccountable tracks
unsettle the mind.

on absence

Gleaming eggs in black sand
– this ancient, patient ritual.

How many of you would crouch
beyond yourselves? Tears

have no place in the kitchen.
One fork. One plate. I used

to hear birds close to morning.
Now asphalt whimpers.

Another disease of the flesh!
Rain & machines collide.

Cherries release their parachutes
– a harvest of stains on the road.

Waiting, what dark will now rise?
Your hand like the curve of an anchor.

Wetlands retreat into deserts.
The steady extinction of tears.

29

A snail among the ashes.
You wake in the night alone.

Who left the candles singing?
The borders of our lives are singed.

I imagine the drastic – always.
A death by the side of the road.

Scars your birth reared darken.
My mind chars anything close.

How will this go much further.
Celan's black milk grows cold.

30

In a dream, we cross the ocean.
Night does not indicate triumph.

So long since I held you sleeping.
Years. (Years). Years.

A poem by de la Mare   he
laced with the word *silver.*

This cannibal grief of motherhood
– when will it be assuaged?

Words like fruits know seasons
Yet seasons have begun to collide.

31

for John Thompson (1938–1976)

A curiously-swirled stone
Flowers who never knew you

: death by choking on absence.
Translation – the impossible act.

Many pencils. Many guns. Many
beer bottles. A farrago of ends.

Lear on the moor with his *never,*
never, never ...

Did you hear him on the Tantramar?
Something broken.

Blessure: wound Blessing: how
you stand in the doorway

and bring me poems. What?
Yes. You. At the edge of the desert,

the last of your secrets
are drowned.

32

for my all-too-gullible heart

The sky is never cluttered with light
Why then do the dark parts hold me?

Your skin, sour as black limes, soft
as undersea, sweet as a line unbidden.

Kunitz felt the slap stinging
in his 64th year. If you asked

me for everything, would I consider it
for a moment? The body grows heavy.

Faces multiply.
Naked, you retract your nakedness.

Too late! Who can understand a door
with many windows?

A yes echoing from the past
becomes a visitor.

In the garden, you find sear marks
from forgetting.

33

after a panic attack

Night. Night. Night.
Who has conveyed me here?

My heart is spinning a web
– catch the darkness. Catch it.

You are still flesh by my side
but the planets of your eyes

are sealed. I reach from a terrible
distance. See the child dropping out of my palm!

On the sill, our life is ranged sightless.
I count goats that ravage

the hillside. A night bird cries by the pear tree.
Unanswerable traffic of the mind.

on catching a glimpse

A room when the lights thin out
– the loneliness in your body.

Baker & Fitzgerald. Candles
like human stars.

There is nothing I can do
about you standing there.

How long has it been, my child?
A bird's nest clutches my throat.

My hands become trees in winter.
At night, I dream like crazy.

A whole solar system of faces.
The moon's an endangered egg

– Ketilsson's boot hanging over it.
Perhaps you'll pass into darkness

The quick intimacy of strangers.
Life sieved through these spaces

Don't ask
I'm made of echoes.

35

anniversary
        for C.N.

Garage doors slam on harvests
– we pick mouthfuls of neglect.

Crows conversing at daybreak
I will never speak their language.

Yes, I have been unfaithful.
Yes, I have sculpted regret.

Miller's story of the clown
you read to me by the creek.

Seven years of traveling.
Do you think the signs will brighten?

There is this – our walks at evening
Fruit breaking from cement.

at the start of the rainy season

Fading beneath my skin
– the land's sharp entrance.

If I should see you again –
will I?

Tomatoes finally turn,
the earth becomes porous

 : on the lake, frayed swans.
Dream of blood dark as eyes,

pretenders to your throne.
Keats' mellow season.

You slip something in my hand,
time's lame address –

what kind of rain
grows inside me.

40th Ghazal – 4 a.m.
for Frank Bonneville

Dark – how it holds me.
A story you tell me of miracles

Salt rising inside your mouth.
Dream of ravens – their kleptomania.

Sid's ashes in the scripture.
Debris.

No moon but a scarred one.
3 lidless stars. You smolder

against my flesh – an instant.
Where are you,

where
are you taking me?

Eyes confess only to absence.
Mona Lisa in the trash.

Points of light & shadow
converging.

38

In my mind, your face dissolves.
Giant on its stem, the sunflower

spills & nods in the wind.
I find a bruise you left behind

in my pocket – rub it like a stone,
blistering. You have not come to call.

The dislocation of poetry: pods
leaving the node: a street scene of needles.

Skittering heart, sore
as the impossible. It's not

that I don't love you,
it's just that

39

without promises

A moth in the smallest room
– we spend our lives as dust.

As though I could live on silence,
knowing nothing but your flesh.

Wind in the last tall trees; cones
with no soil to harbour them.

What do I want to endure.
Montale's flower on the cliff.

You ask me again for commitment
– lips swollen far beyond speech.

40

without entitlement

Where my wedding ring was, a scar
– the sun's faint marriage.

Crucify yourself on a whim!
Too long since bird song mattered.

Giddy again: then weeping
Upended range of weather.

What can I tell you this time?
Words have infinite faces.

The thinnest moon's transparency
Vows contract & explode.

41

A wasp in the clover's mouth.
I have always longed for engulfment

Nostalgia undresses your tongue
The slow, strained music of loss.

Who truly can see the sun?
You still open my body to violence.

Your house unravels around you
– things become things again.

Lips and a roiling of swallows
There's nothing so absent as love.

42

I have not let you ripen.
Afraid there is no end.

Walk in my flesh – I find you –
a tight, sunless garden

whose words are going to seed.
Coiled around desire

– the difference being nothing.
Repeat this a hundred times

: Nijinsky & Gide danced sideways.
And still I see your face

threadbare: young: foreign. The familiar
in my movement (my tongue outside of speech).

on a wizened green plum

Uncreate me!
I have fallen in love with the mad.

Quick steps on the roadway
– Crazy Jane with blackberries between her dugs.

My neck is so small. So small …
Who wept that at the guillotine?

Ann Boleyn's velvet underdress,
seven guilders in a loaf of bread,

wine with the taste of footprints.
Catching like an animal in your sanity,

he, embodied by darkness.
Staring after him, you see a crow

pecking on tin. Zarathustra!
Shelley's Last Man. Redeeming the world

an absence at a time. *Je suis.*
Tu es. Il est. Nous sommes …

A nun strides down my spine,
reciting from a wizened green plum.

44

sister

for Deirdre

By a moment, you are younger.
Years that pass in chasms.

Brutish against your presence
– you small usurper of blonde!

Abba & Piaf on the stereo
Do you recall our cannibal dances?

Nails as claws in the bedroom;
fists as love in the hall.

There was a poet for stopping the war
who'd thrust his hand in a fire if he had to.

That dark touch I would soon cease
if – sister – you spoke a slow flame.

45

turning inside-out

Break me of this burning!
I ache into Medea again,

trade Bachean urges for tears.
Night's slow absolution.

Understood: a wedding ring,
keys for the wounds in your palm.

I can't concentrate on apocalypse.
As if all the birds had died.

When do you watch the earth's
soft openings anymore?

from another room

Four hours of dreaming
: wine & flesh collide.

Thieves tossing dice
for his garments. A wilderness

of hands. *Softly,* you tell me,
softly. The poem is a guiltless

child. I have nothing left
but sounds – grapes

tightening in the sun. What
remains for you to offer me.

Distance stinging
between your words.

47

in limbo

Who have I become
No longer being child

– trying to retrace a lost chasm.
In the earth, our bulbs unfold,

food throbs on my tongue, paper
on the floor in knots.

Just a phony clown show, spewing
Lucky's facts – where, or otherwise,

is the truth? Books sit heavy
without love. I have pledged to you

a word. Now receding
like a flood inside a cavern.

48

on a translation of Rilke's

That fearful, ripening and enormous Being
– once again, sleep grips my mind.

On his arm, the word Nothing
Thought prolongs its absence.

A spider inside a rose petal
Threads of music I've kept tuneless.

Chaos, as such, creates little
– you keep rolling its globe in your throat.

A crow turning keys with its cawing
For a moment, you become stone.

What is the want in your darkness?
To be touched and held and broken.

49

Something begins to be born
– a poem's successful neon.

Flattered by emptiness – gut wrench!
How you've danced upon eyes & eyes.

Robins at dusk in the bushes
(This time. Yes. Be present)

What have they cast aside?
I'm storing your face in my silence.

(Bird cages) (Armor) (Logos)
Ways of containing the nameless.

We walk and we walk in our shadows
You, somehow, still loving the shade.

50

about endings
> *Behind the pain, the poem*
> *Helene Cixous*

Your dark face always shifting
The laugh of a car over gravel

– there is not much, without you, I can feel.
Sour oranges in my stomach,

sun groveling by the clouds.
A room I've stayed before, only smaller.

What has this anger broken?
Years of lies like eggs

– absence now hatching inside them.
I can't reassemble our past

That perfect weep over abortions.
Plastic & metal spawn feathers.

Dry time
– death drawing its bones.

51

without touching
for F. B.

Raven & the day moon
Darkness finally breaking

As if my hands were acid
Scoring entries in your flesh.

A column of Tang on the counter
: the white innards of your fridge: nothing

in your room but questions.
What promise erases this gaze?

Only a fire would answer.
Trakl let poison decide.

Light in the aging lilac
– you leave to remain in the world.

always

A broom held by absence sweeping
– leaves the same colour as litter.

In my dream, your eyes are seeds
Sprouting inside themselves.

Renegade fruit starts ripening
You pack & you pack your brokenness.

What apologies belong to affection?
I have swallowed my hunger this distance.

Perhaps, in a year, or never.
Motion, not place, is your home.

53

In all the world of shoes, I look at one crow.
An ache of leaves on asphalt,

so much loam desires beneath!
Faces eroded by emptiness.

Is there a word I can exit you with?
She irons his lies in the bedroom

– letters & grief pile up.
A silhouette grins like a mother.

I have hands that remember each mouth.
The Pistols. The Pogues & Biafra.

Buses on Hastings in grayness.
Notes dark in a world of dry noise.

then

for C.N.

Missing you, I miss myself
gone missing. Finding other ways

to wake the day. In the pines, raven's
ghost-croak, nuts on maps beneath the road.

Wilderness. Its semblances.
Why am I devoured inside my mind?

Sin's dogs were nothing to this ache.
As bruises in frames,

his pictures, darkening.
So portage over emptiness!

Shadows stirring in the bedroom.
Someone waits who nearly waited from the word.

Afterword

Day of the Dead, 6 p.m., your breath
the only sound in the room, small, this breath

By the overpass, a forest slashed down, crow-wrath
dark overhead, faltering, losing breath

Last firecrackers blast a smoky wreath
– cat darts beneath the hedge, nearly breathless

Where has he gone? You've written his death
yet something still aches – no face, no breath

So many words, the moon's thin white faith
Catherine, you won't stop – but at least   take a breath

Richmond, BC
November 2005